Bria's Bed & Breakfast for Pets Only

Cindy Stewart

Trilogy Christian Publishers
A Wholly Owned Subsidiary of Trinity Broadcasting Network
2442 Michelle Drive
Tustin, CA 92780

Cover design by: Cornerstone Creative Solutions

For information, address Trilogy Christian Publishing
Rights Department, 2442 Michelle Drive, Tustin, Ca 92780.
Trilogy Christian Publishing/ TBN and colophon are trademarks of Trinity Broadcasting Network.

For information about special discounts for bulk purchases, please contact Trilogy Christian Publishing.

Manufactured in the United States of America

10 9 8 7 6 5 4 3 2 1

Library of Congress Cataloging-in-Publication Data is available.

ISBN 978-1-64773-724-5 (Print Book)
ISBN 978-1-64773-725-2 (ebook)

I dedicate this book to all the children in the world. I hope it will bring a smile to their face and show God's love for them.

ria's Bed & Breakfast for Pets Only is a fun and exciting vacation spot for family pets. Families bring their pets here from all over the United States. It is an old Victorian home that is three stories. It sits high on a cliff and has a beautiful view overlooking the ocean. You can see the beach if you stand near the edge of the large yard. The house has a wrap-around porch with comfy chairs and cushions all around so wherever you stand or sit, you have a beautiful view.

Bria is the owner of the B&B. The house has been in her family for generations, and it was left to her from her mama and daddy. Bria grew up in the B&B and has always called it home. As far back as she can remember, her parents have been inviting pets into their home.

Alex and Shakespear live with Bria. They are the house dogs, and they have many responsibilities. Shakespear, being from the take-charge sheep dog family, keeps things in order. Alex, a feisty Yorkshire Terrier, pretty much does what Shakespear says. Alex always tells everyone that he does not mind doing what Shakespear says because Shakespear was living here before he was born. He has never steered him wrong yet, he loves him, and he is his best friend.

This particular day, the house was bubbling with excitement as they prepare for the arrival of their guests and make plans for what lies ahead of them. It was Christmas Eve, and Bria had the house all decorated. The outside was covered with tiny white lights trimming the house and the windows. She had placed greenery everywhere inside, over the doors, and around the windows, and she had tucked gingerbread dog bones all throughout the greenery. She hung candy cane pet treats all over the house. If the guests could reach them, they could eat them.

Bria always liked to do one last check of the guests' rooms to make sure everything is perfect for their guests' arrival. She always wanted to make things extra special for them since they were spending Christmas away from their families. Dog mints were placed on the bed pillows, and each room had baskets of chew toys and rawhides. It made Alex's mouth water looking at all those treats. There were bath powders and cologne sprays in all the baths so the guests can pamper themselves.

As they checked the last bath, Alex pinched his nose and looked up at Shakespear and said, "I think these cologne sprays stink! Shakespear, why do the guests even take baths while they are here on vacation? Seems to me, not having to take a bath should be part of your vacation. I hate it when Bria gives me a bath."

"Well," Shakespear said, "If she didn't make you take a bath like you should, you would stink so bad no one could stand to be around you. Most humans take a bath every day, so count yourself lucky, and like Bria always says, 'Cleanliness is next to godliness.'"

"Well, it may be, but I still hate it," Alex said as he walked out the door.

Everything was in its place. As they walked down the hall, Bria stopped at the front door. "Let us say a prayer before our guests arrive. Dear God, we want to thank You for our guests that are coming to visit us. Please keep them safe and comfort them as they are apart from their families. Thank you for guiding myself, Shakespear, and Alex to make their visit fun, exciting, and a great memory. To You be all the glory and praise. Amen." Bria then turned to Alex and Shakespear. "Now the two of you can go wait on the porch. Let me know when they get here."

Shakespear went out first, and Alex followed right behind him. They were standing looking out at the beautiful view when Shakespear said, "God sure blessed us with a beautiful morning."

"He sure did," Alex said. "Shakespear, I asked Bria this question a while back. How do I pray to Jesus? She told me all I had to do is talk to Him like a friend because He is our friend. She said that God loves everyone because He created us, which means He loves me too, and that if I ask God to show me His blessings, He will."

Shakespear, looking down at Alex, patted him on his head and said, "He sure does love you, little buddy, and He sure will show you. Always remember to thank God for those blessings."

"I do thank Him, and I talk to Him all the time. You know, the first song I ever learned was 'Jesus Loves Me.'" Alex proceeded to break into song. "*Jesus loves me this I know, for the Bible tells me so, little ones to Him belong, they are weak, but He is strong. Yes, Jesus loves me, Yes, Jesus loves me, Yes, Jesus loves me, The Bible tells me so.* I think there is another verse to it, but I can't remember how it goes."

When Alex looked back at the yard, he saw the longest black stretch limousine he had ever seen driving up the winding driveway. Their first guest had arrived. Her name is Ms. FiFi Michelle, a French poodle from Connecticut. When the door to that big black car opened, out shot a little white poodle, yapping as loud as she could. She was all over the place. Ms. FiFi ran all around the yard, then up onto the porch yapping nonstop and almost knocking Alex down.

"Shakespear, what in the world is the matter with her? She's acting crazy, and I can't understand a word she is saying."

Shakespear said, "I'm pretty sure that is French, and some French poodles are very high strung. This is definitely one of them."

In a panic, Alex belted out, "French! I do not speak French! How am I going to talk to her and know what she needs?"

"Calm down," Shakespear said, "She may be able to speak English, too. It wouldn't hurt you any to try to learn some French while she is here."

Just about that time, Ms. FiFi rounded the porch where they were. Before she could get past them, Shakespear turned in front of her. He let out one deep bark and stopped her in her tracks. She was so shocked Alex thought she was going to swallow her tongue. Ms. FiFi straightened up, made one small peep, and did not say another word. "You can follow me," Shakespear said as they walked her into the house. She followed behind as they led the way. She had the look of surprise on her face when she saw all the decorations.

When they arrived at her room, she just stood in the doorway taking in all the pretty furniture and the frills everywhere. Her room had a lace-covered canopy bed with lace-covered pillows scattered all around the room. The room fit Ms. FiFi perfectly. As she stood there, she said in English, "I never expected that it would be so beautiful." She shot into the room and landed in the middle of that bed before either of them knew it. Alex looked up at Shakespear with the biggest look of relief because he had understood what Ms. FiFi had just said.

"I will say this about her: she's quick." Shakespear said to Alex as he turned to Ms. FiFi.

"You make yourself comfortable. Alex and I will be back later." He closed the door behind them.

When Alex and Shakespear returned to the front porch, the limousine had left. Alex was just about to walk down the front steps when this beat-up New York City cab pulled up in front. It rattled and smoked until it finally came to a stop. The door came open on the cab, but no one got out. The driver went around to the passenger side, and they could see him pulling and tugging on something. Finally, Mr. Otis Bunker, a bull dog from New York City, got out of the car. He did not look happy to be there, and he was slobbering all over himself.

Alex said to Shakespear, "He doesn't look too happy to be here. And what's wrong with him? He looks like he is foaming at the mouth."

"Bull dogs do that," Shakespear said.

Alex blurted out, "Well, the place is going to be a mess if he keeps that up all over the house."

"Let's hope that once he's settled, he'll stop doing that," Shakespear said.

Finally, Otis's owner was able to get him to the front porch. Shakespear told Otis to follow him. As they walked through the house towards Otis's room, he was slobbering all the way. Alex noticed Otis was not interested in the decorations at all like Ms. FiFi had been. His room had been decorated in red and green plaid pillows all around with a seat in front of the bay window that overlooked the ocean. It was a beautiful view. When they arrived at his room, he just went right in and laid down on the bed, not saying a word to either of them. "You get some rest. I know that was a long ride from New York City. Get settled in and we'll be back for you later," Shakespear told him as he closed the door behind him.

Alex and Shakespear headed toward the kitchen where Bria had the breakfast trays of gourmet food ready for them to deliver. Breakfast is always extra special at Bria's. Today, she has prepared Puppy Paw Pancakes covered in beef bacon syrup with a side dish of liver-flavored strips. She also added an extra treat, Kitty Kat Parfait, for dessert. Alex and Shakespear love it when there are guests in the house because they are also able to enjoy the delicious food.

Ms. FiFi's room was their first stop. She was so excited to see the tray of food and how Bria had made everything so pretty. Bria had placed a vase of flowers on each tray, and each had pretty cloth napkins to add a special touch.

When they arrived at Otis's room, he seemed to be in the same shape he was in when they left him earlier. He did not even seem to care about the food. Shakespear set the tray down and said, "I'll be right back." Alex was right behind him because he knew Shakespear was up to something. "I think I know what might cheer this fellow up," Shakespear said. "There is a box of toys Bria keeps in the hall closet for the guests. I remember seeing one I think would be perfect for him."

They found the closet and Shakespear rummaged through that box for what seemed like forever until he pulled out a huge rubber yellow cab. Alex jumped up in the air and said, "It doesn't say New York City on it, but it looks about as beat-up as the one he rode up in."

They headed back to Otis's room. "Hey, Otis," Shakespear said, "We found something that we think will make you feel better."

"I don't think anything could make me feel better right now," Otis answered.

When Otis raised his head and saw that beat-up yellow cab Shakespear was holding, he perked up and jumped off the bed. He kept saying, "Thank you, thank you." "You're welcome," Shakespear said. "We thought it might make you feel more at home. You enjoy your breakfast and we will see you later." Shakespear turned and looked down at Alex and said, "See, Alex? It is the little things that can make a person feel comfortable. Sometimes you need to look at things from another person's point of view. Otis is used to seeing yellow cabs all the time, and I think having that toy with him will make him feel less homesick."

After breakfast, Alex and Shakespear rounded up Ms. FiFi and Otis. Bria explained the rules of the house—where they were allowed in the house, mealtimes, and bedtime. She also told them they could eat any treats they could reach but to remember mealtime is always fantastic around here and to try not to ruin their appetites. Bria patted Shakespear on the head and said, "Take our guests down to the beach to play for a while."

They were headed out the door when Ms. FiFi shot past them and headed for the beach. Shakespear said, "Come on, we need to get to her before she hurts herself. She doesn't know this area well." Alex and Otis took off behind him.

The pathway down the cliff to the beach has the most beautiful view. There are all kinds of wildflowers that line the zigzagged path. All the different colors of flowers add so much beauty to the side of the cliff. Rock platforms jet out to the side of the path where the guests, should they feel like it, can stop and relax. They can enjoy the view, listen to the waves and seagulls, and warm their bones.

When they finally made their way down the path to the beach, Ms. FiFi and Otis were both surprised at the amusement park they had built for them right there on the beach. They had a carousel, a basket ride, a Ferris wheel, and even games to play. Shakespear runs the rides, and Alex helps with the games.

Otis headed straight for the Ferris wheel. He said he wanted to get up high so he could see everything at once. He was used to sitting in a cab and looking at tall buildings all around him all the time. This was really an adventure for him.

Ms. FiFi spotted the basket ride and immediately wanted to get on it. Shakespear knew that she was too small for the ride and that it would scare her, so he kept trying to persuade her to ride the carousel or play some of the games instead. He even walked off trying to ignore her, which was impossible because she took every step he took, yapping French at him. Finally, after he had enough, he turned to her and said, "Okay, I am going to let you ride it, but I really don't feel it is a good idea. It is really scary up there, and there are reasons they have rules." Ms. FiFi immediately said, "I'm not scared one bit." She proceeded to climb into the wire basket. Shakespear closed the door on the wire basket she was in and latched it.

Alex looked up at Shakespear and said, "This I gotta see. I won't even get on that ride and I'm the bravest Yorkshire Terrier that I know."

"You don't know any other Yorkshire Terriers," Shakespear replied.

"Well, if I did, I know I would be the bravest."

Shakespear knew he could control the ride and made it go slow so Ms. FiFi would not get hurt. He hoped this ride would teach her a lesson. He pushed the power button on the basket ride, and it started to move. When Ms. FiFi's basket started to move up into the air, they heard the loudest scream they had ever heard come out of her, "Get me out of here!" At least, that is what it sounded like she was saying, but it was hard to tell. She was so scared that she was mixing her English and French. As her basket came around to Alex and Shakespear, they could see Ms. FiFi clinging to the door of the basket. One would have thought she had some cat in her the way she was hanging on.

Alex asked Shakespear, "How long are you going to make her ride it?"

"Long enough to teach her that she needs to learn to listen and follow the rules. There are reasons for rules."

When Ms. FiFi's basket came around the next time, Shakespear stopped the ride. Alex reached up and opened the door to which Ms. FiFi was still clinging. She slowly slid to the ground and just sat there.

"You alright?" Alex asked. She just looked up at him and nodded her head.

"Good," Alex said. "Let's go play some of the games. I think you'll like those better."

"That sounds like a really good idea," she said. "And Shakespear, I know now why there are rules. I don't want to feel like that ever again." She came to her feet and off she and Alex went.

Alex took Ms. FiFi over to the shell and pea game booth. This was his favorite game of all because he got to play with the guest. As he moved those three shells around, Ms. FiFi tried to guess which shell the pea was under. She was getting more and more excited, yet frustrated, because she kept picking the wrong shell. She was just about to give up when Alex said, "Let's try one more time." He started moving the shells around, and when he stopped, she picked the one in the center. Alex asked her, "Are you sure that is the one you want to pick?" "Yes," she said. Alex lifted the shell in the center and set the pea under it. Ms. FiFi got so excited that she reached up, grabbed that pea, and stuck it up her nose. Alex looked at her in shock and said, "What did you go and do that for? I need that pea for the game! Though I am not so sure I want it back. You need to get that out of your nose right now." She reached up and tried to remove the pea, but it would not budge. Alex told her to blow hard, but that did not work either. Finally, Alex said, "This is just awful, I have to go get Shakespear. You stay right here and keep blowing!"

Alex headed toward Shakespear, who was letting Otis off the Ferris wheel. As Alex got to Shakespear, he said in a panic, "Shakespear, Ms. FiFi stuck the pea up her nose!"

"She did what?" Shakespear asked.

"Yeah, she went and grabbed that pea and stuck it up her nose. Who does that?" Alex blurted out.

"Come on, let's see what is going on here," Shakespear said.

"Shouldn't we go get Bria?" Alex asked.

"Whoa! Whoa! Whoa! I am in charge. I'll try to fix it first, and then I'll tell Bria." Shakespear answered in his take-charge voice.

Otis spoke up and said to Alex, "She really stuck a pea up her nose?"

"As sure as I'm standing here. I have never seen anything like it. Who does that?"

"Well, this I gotta see," Otis said.

They followed Shakespear over to where Ms. FiFi was. She was still blowing hard out of her nose, but that pea was not moving. Shakespear stood there thinking to himself for a few minutes. "I'll be right back. I've got an idea."

It was not long before Shakespear came back. He had brought a can of black pepper with him. He told Ms. FiFi that she should sniff the pepper and try to sneeze. He poured some in his paw and had her sniff it. She took a big sniff, but nothing happened. Then they heard a little prissy peep of a sneeze.

"She's going to have to do better than that," Alex said. Alex then shot a prayer up to God saying out loud, "Lord, please let that pea come out of her nose."

They heard the loudest sneeze come out of Ms. FiFi, and that pea shot out like a slingshot. It flew across the walkway, and with a loud ping, it hit the bullseye in the softball throwing booth and ricocheted off to who knows where.

Alex looked up. "Thank You, Lord!"

He turned to Shakespear and said, "What are the chances of that? I cannot hit that bullseye when I am standing right in front of it! Just to let you know, if you should find that pea, I do not want it back now that it has been up Ms. FiFi's nose. Gross!" Shakespear asked Ms. FiFi if she was okay, and she replied that she was. They headed back to the house just as Bria was calling them for dinner. Perfect timing.

They always ate dinner in the formal dining room when guests were there. Bria had decorated the table and the room; it looked so pretty. She had prepared the best meal for them. They were having filet with liver-flavored gravy, and for dessert, they were going to have Puppy Paw ice cream. After everyone was seated, Bria said the blessing. "Thank You, Lord, for this food You give us, and thank You for our guests. Thank You for all Your many blessings. In Jesus Christ, our Lord, we pray." Together they all said a hearty "amen."

It was a very enjoyable meal together. Otis and Ms. FiFi kept talking about their day and how much fun they had.

They were all so stuffed after dinner that they just went in the living room and lay down. Otis spoke up and said, "You guys sure do eat some fancy food around here. My usual meal is hot dogs."

Alex perked up and said, "Hot dogs!"

He ran over to Otis, "I want to hear more about those hot dogs."

"Well," Otis said, "You can buy them right off the street."

"Right off the street?" Alex asked.

"Yeah. They have carts set up, and you can get anything you want on your hot dog."

"Anything?" Alex asked.

"Yep, anything."

"I sure would like to try one of those someday," Alex said.

"You haven't had a good hot dog until you have had one from New York City," Otis said, grinning from ear-to-ear.

It was not long before Bria came in and surprised them when she sat down at the piano and said, "Since it is Christmas Eve, we're going to sing some Christmas carols. Who wants to go first?"

They must have sung every Christmas carol they knew before it was time to go to bed. Before they headed to bed, they said their prayers. Bria explained to Ms. FiFi and Otis that every night they always say something for which they are grateful. She explained how we should be grateful for what God gives us, especially the small things. She started with herself and said, "I am very grateful for all of you." Shakespear went next and said that he was grateful for the sunshine today. Ms. FiFi said she was grateful to get to come to such a pretty place, and Otis said he was grateful for the yellow cab Shakespear had given him. Alex looked deep in thought when he said, "I'm grateful for the Puppy Paw ice cream we ate for dessert!"

Ms. FiFi had everyone up early the next day with her yapping. It was Christmas morning. After Shakespear and Alex had delivered the breakfast trays, and they had all eaten, they met in the living room. Everyone was wishing each other a merry Christmas. Alex jumped up and said, "Happy birthday, Jesus!"

Bria patted him on his head and said, "That's right! It is Jesus' birthday. What a perfect thing to say, and we also want to thank God for the gift of His Son."

"And that is the best gift of all," Alex said.

Bria finally announced, "It's time to open our presents."

They were all so excited. She handed Ms. FiFi her gift first. Bria had made her a white sweater with rhinestones around the collar.

"Oh, Bria, I just love it! And look how pretty I look in it."

Bria had knitted Otis a green sweater and she had embroidered the words "I Love New York" on it. A tear glistened in the eye of the big, gruff, no-nonsense Otis when he tried it on.

As Shakespear opened his gift and saw that it was a plaid jacket, a big smile spread across his face. "How did you know this is the jacket I have always wanted?" he asked Bria. She smiled and said, "I saw you admiring the one the Irish Setter had at the dog show this past spring, and I knew it would be perfect for you."

Alex was last to open his gift. As he lifted the top of that big box, he got so excited. Bria had made him a blue jean jacket. In one quick move, he put that jacket on, jumped up in the air, and said, "How cool do I look?" He ran over to Bria, and before she knew it, Alex was in her lap kissing her all over her face.

Now it was time for Bria to open her gift. Alex and Shakespear watched closely as Bria opened her present. They had saved their allowance all year to buy her a gold locket. It was heart-shaped with three tiny rhinestones in the center, and it opened to reveal a picture of Alex and Shakespear on each side. When she unwrapped it, Bria was so touch by their gift.

When Alex saw her tear up, he asked, "Happy tears?"

She said, "Yes, happy tears, Alex. This is the most beautiful locket; I will cherish it forever. Thank you so much. Well, we better get this paper cleaned up so we can get to the animal shelter."

Every Christmas, they help the homeless animals in their town. They collect rawhides and chew toys. Bria crochets, knits, and sews sweaters for them. She always says they should always give back to the community and share what they have with the less fortunate. Plus, it really does more for the givers than the receivers.

After everyone helped load the car, they were off to the animal shelter. The shelter is located in their small, quaint downtown area. It is like stepping back in time. Some of the streets are still cobblestone from back in the day, and the antique streetlights add a special touch to the area. The people that live in the neighborhood always decorate for the holidays in a big way. Alex and Shakespear always love going down there because they never know what they are going to see.

This year they did not let them down. When they arrived at the animal shelter, it was just beautiful. They sat in the car for a few minutes just to take it all in. The shelter was covered in colorful Christmas lights. Christmas trees all decorated differently lined the sides of the shelter.

"Bria," Alex said, "There must be fifty Christmas trees around that building."

"I think you're right Alex."

Ms. Fifi looked like she was in a trance as she just stared out the window. Otis spoke up, "I have seen a lot of store windows decorated back home, but I have never seen anything like this."

Bria turned the car off and explained the rules, which were simple. Alex and Shakespear had them memorized. You can go anywhere in the room, but you are not allowed to leave the building. As soon as she had finished telling them the rules, Alex looked over at Ms. FiFi. She still looked like she was in a trance staring out the window. "Hey, snap out of it! It's time to go in," Alex said.

They all grabbed some of the presents and headed to the door. Everyone was so glad to see them, and they made them feel so welcome. They had more fun passing out the gifts they had brought. Even Otis and Ms. FiFi helped. Alex and Shakespear were getting to reconnect with old friends. They had run into Pebbles and Molly, two Shih Tzus they had met on Thanksgiving and started catching up with them. Otis was hanging out with a couple of German Shepherds he had met named Thelma and Don. Don had been to New York City, and they had a lot to talk about. It seemed a certain Doberman named Rodner had caught Ms. FiFi's eye, and she was not letting him out of her sight.

Alex and Shakespear set up a table by the front door to pass out candy cane rawhides. They loved this job because they were able to say hi to everyone. It was so good to see their friends.

Things were calm by the door. Alex and Shakespear were just sitting there watching what a good time everyone was having, when Alex jumped up.

"Yippee, there's Aunt Kathy and her dog, Luna."

"How can you tell that is Aunt Kathy and Luna from way over here as crowded as this room is?" Shakespear asked.

"I'd know them anywhere," Alex said. "I stayed with them for two weeks. Remember me telling you about those great treats Aunt Kathy had? She did not mind giving them out, and she gave me treats all day long. Luna thought I was her toy a couple of times while I was there. I have been up close and personal with her. I would know that Goldendoodle anywhere."

Before Shakespear could respond, Alex shot across that room and jumped into Aunt Kathy's arms and started kissing her all over her face.

"I think he is glad to see you," Bria said.

"I think he is too. Merry Christmas, Alex. Where is Shakespear?" Aunt Kathy asked.

"Here he comes," answered Alex.

When Shakespear got to them, Aunt Kathy patted him on his head. "Merry Christmas to you, too, Shakespear. I brought you both something," she said. She held out two gifts, one for each of them. As they opened their gifts, one could tell by the look on their faces that they both liked what they had received. She had given each of them a bag of the treats Alex had mentioned to Shakespear.

Again, in a flash, Alex jumped into Aunt Kathy's arms and started kissing her all over her face. "You're welcome! You're welcome!" she said laughing. They visited with her and Luna for a while and then took Luna around to meet some of their friends.

After a little bit, Bria found Shakespear and told him to round everyone up because they would be leaving soon. Shakespear informed Alex, and Alex took off to find Otis and Ms. FiFi. He found Otis still talking to Don and Thelma and told him they were ready to leave.

"Have you seen Ms. FiFi?" Alex asked.

"Last time I saw her she was talking to Rodner."

"We need to find her. Will you help me look?" asked Alex.

"Sure," Otis said, and they took off in search of her.

Alex took one side of the room and Otis took the other. After searching for some time, they met up and neither of them had found her. "Oh, this is awful," Alex said. "We have to go tell Shakespear."

Off they went to find him. When they got to Shakespear, Alex said, "Shakespear! We can't find Ms. FiFi, we have looked everywhere, she is lost!"

"Who was she seen with last?" Shakespear asked.

"Otis said last time he saw her she was talking to Rodner the Doberman by the backdoor."

"Well, we'll go over there and see if anybody knows anything," Shakespear said. "That girl can't get into more mischief," he murmured to himself.

Alex spoke up, "Shouldn't we tell Bria?"

Shakespear immediately said, "Whoa! Whoa! Whoa! We'll try to find her first, then I'll tell Bria later."

"You sure are going to have a lot to tell her," Alex said as he ran past him.

They headed for the backdoor area and started asking if anyone had seen her. No luck. Finally, Shakespear said, "We'll just go outside and see if she is out there."

"We'll be breaking the rules," Alex said.

"I know, but this one time we need to. We have to see if she is out there," Shakespear answered in his take-charge voice.

Otis went one direction, and Alex and Shakespear went the other. They headed down the street where the shelter was located, looking everywhere she could possibly be, but there was still no sign of her.

"This is awful. We have never lost a guest before," Alex said.

"We haven't lost her. We just can't find her right now," Shakespear said.

"Well, that sounds like we lost her to me!"

"Oh, come on, keep looking," Shakespear said.

They came up on a dark alley. Shakespear looked down at Alex and said, "We need to go in there and look for her."

Alex immediately said, "I'm not going in there."

"We have to. You know how she likes to hide underneath things, and she could be anywhere in there."

"Oh, okay! This wasn't in the job description!" Alex mumbled and slowly started down the alley. "This is one creepy place," Alex whispered to himself.

They looked everywhere they thought she might be, but there was still no sign of her. They decided to go look down the streets that were close to the shelter.

As they were walking out of the dark alley, Alex screamed, "Yuck! Gross!"

"What's the matter?" Shakespear asked as he looked down to see Alex on his tiptoes.

"I just stepped in something gross and it stinks!"

"What did you step in?" asked Shakespear.

"I don't know, it's too dark to see what it is. All I know is I stink! I have to find a water puddle real quick because, if Bria smells me, I will for sure have to take another bath, and I just had one yesterday. I don't want to take another bath," Alex said in a whine.

"Oh, come on, we need to find Ms. FiFi. You are so dramatic," Shakespear said.

Otis was walking past the alley when they walked out towards the street. "I think we should stop right here, and we should say a prayer and ask God to help us find her," said Shakespear. "I think that's a great idea," Alex said.

The three of them stood there and asked God to be with them and to guide them to Ms. FiFi. Then they started up the street looking for her. Alex was looking more for water puddles than he was for Ms. FiFi with no luck because it had not rained for days. They had turned the corner when they heard a small dog barking.

Shakespear spoke up and said, "That's her! I would know that yapping anywhere. I have had to listen to it the last two days."

He was right. They rounded the next corner, and there she was, sitting by Rodner looking in the window of a pet shop. Alex and Shakespear looked up to heaven, and together said, "Thank You, Lord!"

"We should have asked God first," Alex said.

"We sure should have," Shakespear said in agreement.

When they got to her, Shakespear was the first to say something. "We have been looking everywhere for you Ms. FiFi."

"Yeah! I even stepped in something and I don't even know what it was," Alex chimed in.

Shakespear took charge and said, "Why did you run off like that?"

"I couldn't help it, Rodner asked me to go look at the lights at the pet shop," she answered sheepishly.

"Well, you should never leave without telling someone where you are going," Shakespear scolded.

"I'm sorry," Ms. FiFi said.

"Well, okay, but please tell me you won't do that again," he said as he nudged her toward the shelter. "We need to get back because I know Bria is looking for us."

When Bria arrived at the car, they were all standing there, looking innocent as ever. She knew something was up, but she could not put her finger on it. "Where have you all been? I have been looking for you," Bria questioned. Alex went to speak up and Shakespear immediately covered his mouth to muffle what he was going to say. He bent down and whispered in Alex's ear, "I'll tell her later." Alex whispered back, "Well, as soon as she gets a whiff of me, she is going to know for sure we were up to something." They all took their place in the car and no one said a word. As they were headed home, Bria said, "I don't know what you have been up to but I do know that when we get home whoever it is that smells so bad will be getting a bath."

When they arrived at home and the car came to a stop, they started to get out. Immediately, Bria said, "Stay where you are. No one gets out until I figure out where that smell is coming from."

When she got out to come around the car to let Ms. FiFi out, Alex leaned over to Shakespear and said, "There is no way I'm getting out of this."

As she opened the back door where Alex was, she immediately knew where the smell was coming from. "Otis, Shakespear, Ms. FiFi, you can go in the house and start getting ready for bed. Alex, you are coming with me. You need a bath. You stink." As she carried him to the bathroom, all they could hear was Alex yelling, "Save yourselves! Save yourselves!"

"What does he mean 'save yourselves'?" Ms. FiFi asked Shakespear.

"Don't pay any attention to him. He can be very dramatic at times." They each went to their rooms and prepared for bedtime.

Shakespear walked into the bathroom where Bria and Alex were. "We're ready for bed Bria," he said. He could not help but grin a little looking at Alex in the sink because he sure looked pitiful. He was sorry Alex had to get a bath two days in a row, but he had to sleep with him. Alex looked up at Shakespear and said, "I should get workers' compensation for this."

Bria wrapped a towel around Alex, and as she lifted him out of the sink, she said, "Thank you, Shakespear, we'll be there in a few minutes to say our prayers as soon as I blow dry Alex."

Alex thought to himself, *Great, now I have to have five-hundred-mile-per-hour air blown in my face.* It was tough having to take a bath, but he knew that when it was over, Bria would give him lots of kisses and tell him what sweet kisses he had. In the end, it was worth it.

Bria rounded everyone together for their bedtime prayer. As she looked down at all four of them, in a soft voice, she prayed, "Dear God, we have so much to be grateful for today." Alex thought to himself, *You have no idea, Bria.* She prayed, "Thank You that we were able to spend time with good friends, and thank You for what You have given us so that we could share with others. Thank You for keeping us safe. Amen."

They all took turns telling each other what they were grateful for that day. Alex said aloud that he was grateful for Christmas lights, but both he and Shakespear knew deep down they were especially grateful to God for helping them find Ms. FiFi.

Everyone was up early again. Today, the guests would be leaving to go back home to their families. After one last wonderful breakfast at the B&B, Bria presented them with their take-home gift bag. She likes to personalize them for each guest, so they know how special they are to her. She had filled both with homemade gourmet treats.

For Ms. FiFi, she had found the prettiest pink collar and had engraved "Ms. FiFi" on a heart charm that hung from it. She had made Otis a collar and woven "NYC" with a heart beside it and placed it in his bag. After opening their going-away gifts, they both wanted Bria to put their new collars on them. Otis said, "I'll always remember you guys when I wear it."

Shakespear took Otis aside and handed him the yellow cab toy he had given him earlier and said, "You take this with you. No one could appreciate this toy as much as you." Seeing the look on Otis's' face, Shakespear thought to himself, *Bria is right. It is better to give than receive.*

They headed for the front porch to wait for their families to come pick them up. It was hard to see them leave, but Alex and Shakespear did enjoy watching the love between them and their families when they reunited again. Otis turned to Shakespear and said, "You need to come to New York City sometime. I'll show you around."

Alex immediately said, "Can we, Shakespear? I want one of those hot dogs he was talking about."

"We'll have to talk to Bria about that, but if we ever go, we will definitely let you know."

Alex took Otis to the side and said, "Hey Otis, do you think you could mail me one of those hot dogs if I mailed you some of that Kitty Kat parfait you liked so much?"

"That sounds like a great idea, and I'll get the works for you on that hot dog."

Ms. FiFi's long black limousine drove up first, and before they knew it, Ms. FiFi shot across the yard yapping French all the way to the car.

A little while later, Otis's owner drove up in his New York City cab. It was still smoking and rattling as bad as when he had dropped Otis off. Otis perked up and said, "There's my dad!" He ran towards the cab. You could tell they had missed each other so much.

Everyone was now on their way back home, and Alex and Shakespear could rest. They decided to go lay on the porch in two chairs that faced the ocean. The breeze was blowing, and it was the perfect spot to take a nap. As they walked up the steps to the porch, Alex said, "Those sure were two exciting days we had."

"They sure were," Shakespear answered.

"I wonder who will come to visit next and what kind of adventure we'll have," Alex pondered aloud.

"Bria said we have two guests coming to visit next time—a parrot named Mike from Florida and a Yorkshire Terrier like you named Atticus from Tennessee," Shakespear answered as he jumped into the chair in which he had chosen to take his nap.

"Wow," Alex said, "I'll get to meet my first Yorkshire Terrier and talking bird. I bet those two days are going to be exciting."

As they both lay nodding off to nap, Alex said, "Shakespear, I'm going to talk to Bria about getting a baseball team together. We will have plenty to play because there are several dogs from the shelter that want to play. You can coach us. I talked to Samatha, the Siamese cat. She said she would get some of her kitty friends and that they can be the cheerleaders. Otis told me you can get hot dogs at baseball games in New York City. Maybe we can get hot dogs at our games. That would be so great! I hope I can talk Bria into that."

Alex lay there thinking about how he was going to ask Bria about the baseball team when he perked his head up and said, "Hey Shake, you know what's on my grateful list tonight?"

Shakespear responded lazily, "No what?"

Alex answered, "That hot dog! Otis is going to send me one." And then he rolled over on his back and laughed and laughed out loud.

"You are so dramatic," Shakespear said, and then they both nodded off to sleep.

About the Author

Cindy grew up in Tennessee. Her love for God and wanting every child in the world to know that God loves them is what inspired her to write her first children's book. She always gives God the credit for laying this story on her heart and allowing her to be His messenger.

CPSIA information can be obtained
at www.ICGtesting.com
Printed in the USA
BVHW020021120521
607056BV00016B/2005

COBRAS

Michelle Lynch
Trace Taylor

This is a cobra.

Cobras can live here.

Some cobras can be red, white, or black.

They look like where they live.

This cobra looks like the grass.

This cobra looks like the tree.

This cobra looks like the sand.

These are the animals that eat the cobra.

This is the cobra's head.

The head can get big like this.

The cobra head gets big to make animals go.

This is what the cobra likes to eat.

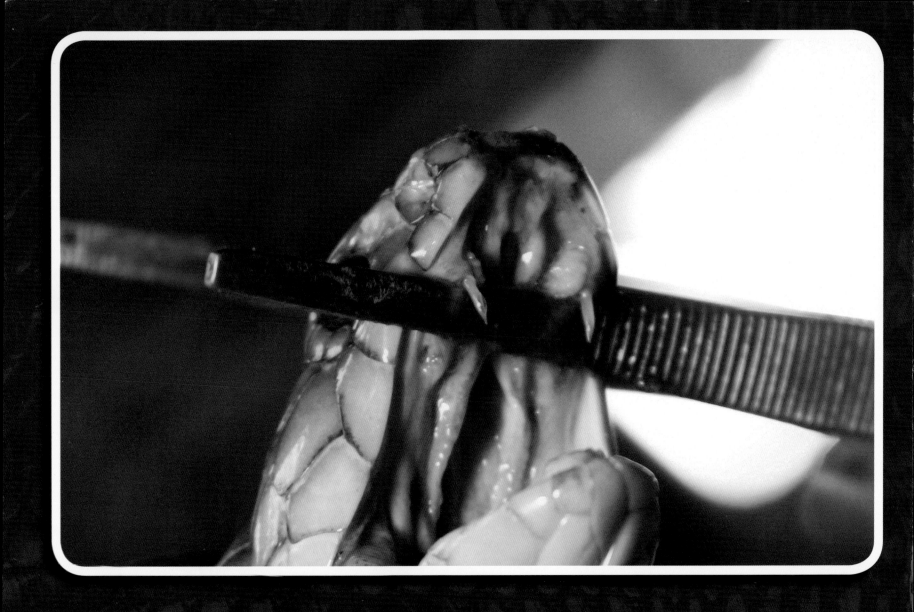

The fangs will go in.

The animal will stop.
Then the cobra will eat.

The cobra is the one snake
that will make a nest.

The babies come out of the eggs.

Cobras live where there are trees.

We take the trees to make
our homes.

There will be no home for the cobra if we take the trees.

Where the Cobra Lives

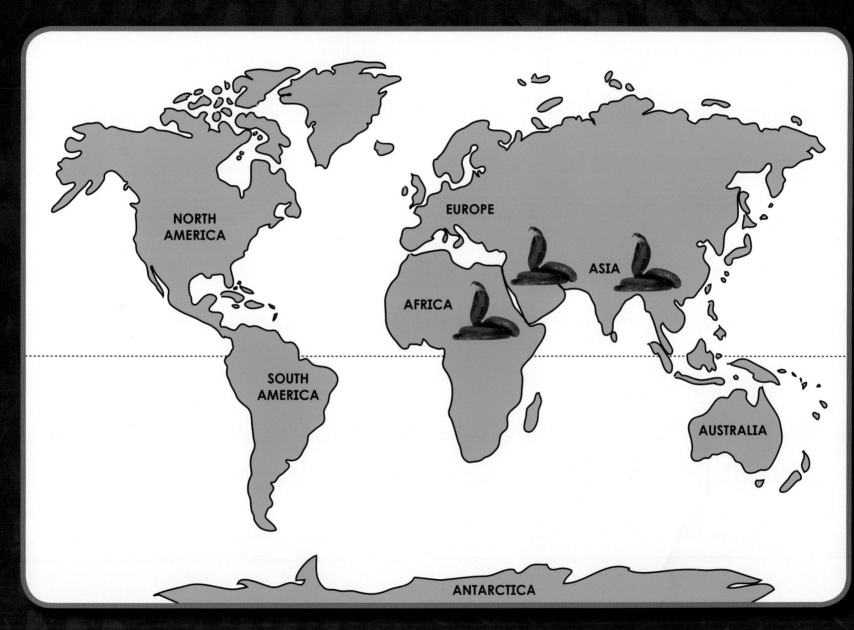

The Cobra's Food Web

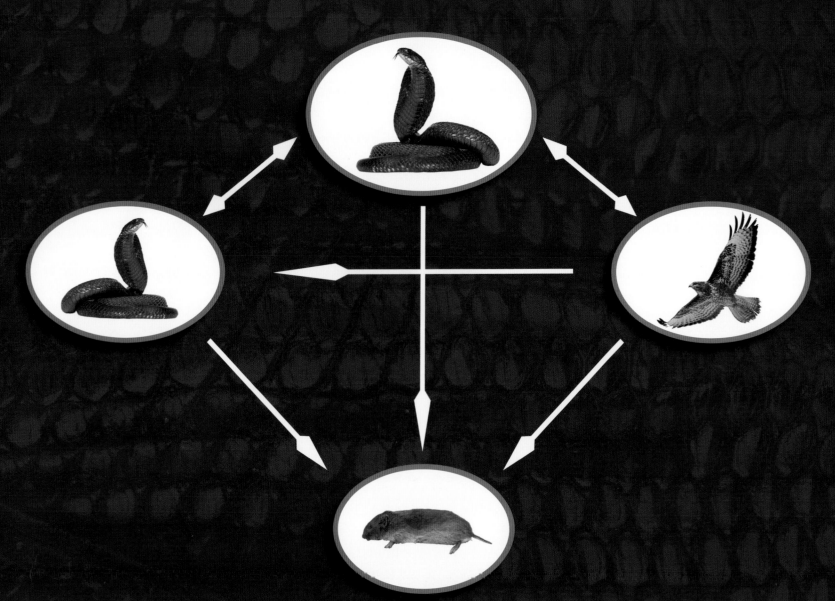

The Cobra's Life Cycle

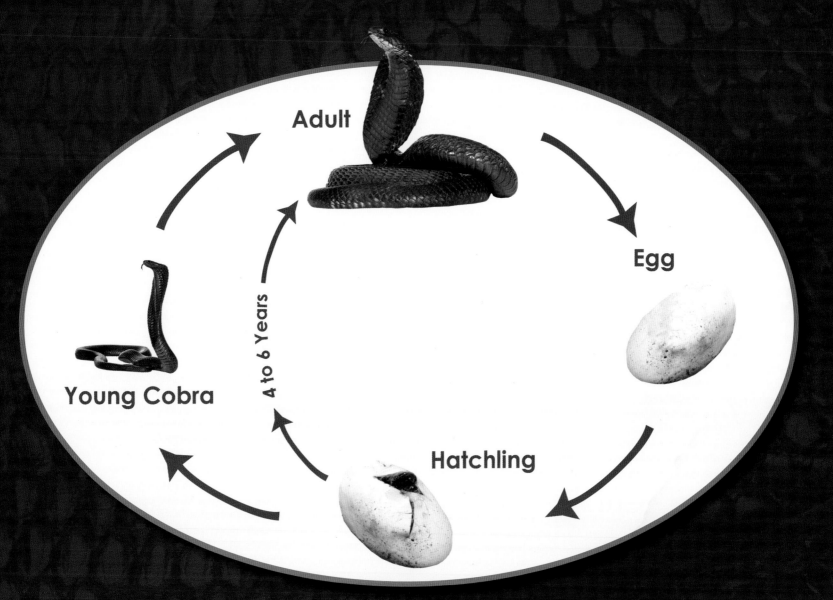

Adult

Egg

Hatchling

Young Cobra

4 to 6 Years

Power Words
How many can you read?

animal	can	here	look	our	that	to
are	come	home	make	out	then	we
baby	eat	if	no	red	there	what
be	for	in	of	some	these	where
big	get	like	one	stop	they	white
black	go	live	or	take	this	will

Cobra Words

babies	fangs	head	nest	scales	trees
eggs	grass	hood	sand	snake	water